SHELTER FROM THE TEXAS WINDS

She slipped her arms out of her dress, then reached around his neck. Both had known this moment would come; both knew without asking that it would be impossible to get through this night without acting on their passion, for the feelings were too strong to deny. Both knew this might be all they ever had. The urgency of the moment only brought forth an even greater need.

"I can't see well enough. Let's wash the dust off each other." He pulled her arms from around his neck and helped her out of her dress. He took off her shoes, and she sat there in her bloomers and camisole.

She dipped her hands in the water and soaped them, rubbing them over his face and neck, then dipped one end of the towel into the water. Neither of them spoke as she washed the dirt from him, soaping her hands again and running them over his arms and upper chest. This was only the second time she had seen him or any man, for that matter, bare-chested. She felt both awkward and daring. He took hold of her wrists then and moved her hands down . . .

HISTORICAL ROMANCES BY EMMA MERRITT

RESTLESS FLAMES   (2203, $3.95)

Having lost her husband six months before, determined Brenna Allen couldn't afford to lose her freight company, too. Outfitted as wagon captain with revolver, knife and whip, the single-minded beauty relentlessly drove her caravan, desperate to reach Santa Fe. Then she crossed paths with insolent Logan Mac-Dougald. The taciturn Texas Ranger was as primitive as the surrounding Comanche Territory, and he didn't hesitate to let the tantalizing trail boss know what he wanted from her. Yet despite her outrage with his brazen ways, jet-haired Brenna couldn't suppress the scorching passions surging through her . . . and suddenly she never wanted this trip to end!

COMANCHE BRIDE   (2549, $3.95)

When stunning Dr. Zoe Randolph headed to Mexico to halt a cholera epidemic, she didn't think twice about traversing Comanche territory . . . until a band of bloodthirsty savages attacked her caravan. The gorgeous physician was furious that her mission had been interrupted, but nothing compared to the rage she felt on meeting the barbaric warrior who made her his slave. Determined to return to civilization, the ivory-skinned blonde decided to make a woman's ultimate sacrifice to gain her freedom — and never admit that deep down inside she burned to be loved by the handsome brute!

SWEET, WILD LOVE   (2834, $4.50)

It was hard enough for Eleanor Hunt to get men to take her seriously in sophisticated Chicago — it was going to be impossible in Blissful, Kansas! These cowboys couldn't believe she was a real attorney, here to try a cattle rustling case. They just looked her up and down and grinned. Especially that Bradley Smith. The man worked for her father and he still had the audacity to stare at her with those lust-filled green eyes. Every time she turned around, he was trying to trap her in his strong embrace.

Available wherever paperbacks are sold, or order direct from the Publisher. Send cover price plus 50¢ per copy for mailing and handling to Zebra Books, Dept. 3568, 475 Park Avenue South, New York, N.Y. 10016. Residents of New York, New Jersey and Pennsylvania must include sales tax. DO NOT SEND CASH.

COMANCHE SUNSET

F. Rosanne Bittner

ZEBRA BOOKS
KENSINGTON PUBLISHING CORP.

ZEBRA BOOKS

are published by

Kensington Publishing Corp.
475 Park Avenue South
New York, NY 10016

First printing: November, 1991

Printed in the United States of America

FROM THE AUTHOR . . .

Fort Stockton, the location of most of the events in this story, was located in west Texas, approximately eighty miles south of New Mexico. It was the primary camp for soldiers sent west to guard travelers and supplies along the route of the San Antonio-San Diego Stage Line in the 1850's and 60's before the Southern Pacific railroad was built. This roadway is actually a section of the better-known Old Spanish Trail, which ran all the way from Florida to California.

Fort Stockton was originally established as Saint Gall, a center for Jesuit Priests in 1845. It became a fort in 1854 after the Guadalupe-Hidalgo treaty with Mexico, in which the U.S. agreed to keep raiding Comanche out of Mexico. Part of the reason for its particular location was an abundant water supply at nearby Comanche Springs.

As in all my books, I prefer to use real historical locations and events in my stories. Although this story does not involve any major historical events, it does cover the situation of the Comanche during this time period, and the general attitude of whites toward these Indians. Regrettably, the hatred between the two cultures was not without foundation on either side; but as in most such cases, those completely innocent of wrongdoing often suffered the brunt of that hatred.

I might also point out that my depiction of the situation and the character of the soldiers at Fort Stockton in this story are totally fictitious, and are based on the general situations and attitudes that existed at western outposts during this time period, a matter of historical record.

All characters in this novel, and the details involving their lives, are fictitious and a product of this author's imagination.

Do you know when they will crouch down and bring their young into the world? In the wilds their young grow strong . . .
I gave them the desert to be their home,
And let them live on the salt plains . . .
No one can tame them . . .
They do not know the meaning of fear,
And no sword can turn them back.

Job 39:3, 4, 6, 7, 22